W9-BNV-531

2005
Dear Patrick,
Hope you enjoy
the book!
Love
Aidan

This book belongs to:

Patrick Larkin McGrath

Please be kind to this book!

Translated by Laura Lindgren

Copyright © 1994 by Coppenrath Verlag, 48155 Münster, Germany.
First published in Germany under the title *Briefe von Felix*.
English translation copyright © 1994 by Parklane Publishing. All rights reserved.
First published in the United States and Canada in 1994 by Abbeville Press.
Reissued in 2003 by Parklane Publishing,
a division of Book Club of America Inc., Hauppauge, New York.
ISBN 1-59384-034-9 / Printed in Hong Kong
1 3 5 7 9 10 8 6 4 2

LETTERS FROM FELIX

A Little Rabbit on a World Tour

Story by Annette Langen
Illustrations by Constanza Droop

PARKLANE PUBLISHING

HAUPPAUGE, NEW YORK

Departures ←

A

Mom

Sophie

Lena

At the end of vacation something terrible happened. Suddenly, in the middle of the airport, Sophie's cuddly rabbit Felix disappeared. "Don't worry, Sophie," Mom reassured her and put her arm around her. But Sophie felt a big lump in her throat. "What if Felix is lost forever and ever?" she thought.

INFORMATIO

KLM	125	AMSTERDAM
AF	1263	PARIS
AA	3107	NEW YORK
JA	7053	TOKYO
FA	2904	HELSINKI
AA	268	SYDNEY
BA	4028	LONDON
SAS	364	STOCKHOLM
LH	5174	BRUSSELS
AI	2215	ROME

Dad

Julius

"I'll find him," Dad promised and started looking right away.

"We'll help too," her brothers and sister added.

But even though Lena, Nicolas, Julius, Sophie, and Dad ran all around looking and asked everyone they met, the little rabbit was nowhere to be found.

Nicolas

This was very, very bad! Sophie and Felix had known each other forever, or at least since they had snuggled together in Sophie's crib. And even when Sophie grew bigger, Felix still got to sleep in the bed. The little cuddly rabbit and Sophie were inseparable. Only when she went to school did he have to wait for her at home. And every afternoon she would tell Felix exactly what had happened at school. They shared everything! Sophie was sure that Felix loved spaghetti more than anything just as she did. Felix always understood Sophie, and Sophie knew what Felix wanted to say to her.

When it was time for their plane to leave, there still wasn't the slightest trace of Felix. And so Sophie had to board the plane without her cuddly rabbit. She didn't want extra ice cream or the seat by the window. She just sat sadly.

To cheer Sophie up, her little sister, Lena, drew a rabbit with crayons for her. He did look a little like her lost Felix. Sophie swallowed hard and swallowed again, and then a tear and more tears ran down her cheeks.

Back home at bedtime, the bed seemed scary and empty without Felix. And so the summer vacation came to a sad end.

School begins again today. But Sophie isn't even looking forward to seeing her friends and her favorite teacher. All she can think about is poor Felix. He has never traveled alone before—isn't he awfully scared? When the first day of school is over at last, Sophie slowly makes her way home. She doesn't want to think about how there will be no more Felix waiting for her in her room. Her feet grow heavier and heavier, and it takes her a million minutes to reach the garden gate in front of her house. But why is Mom so excited? She is waving something in the air, and she calls, "Sophie, look! There is some mail for you!" Sure enough, there is her name on the envelope. Amazed—who could write in such a squiggly scrawl?—Sophie turns the envelope over.

NEWS FOR
SOPHIE
33 ELM ROAD
MANSFIELD, OHIO
U.S.A.

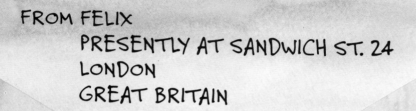

FROM FELIX
PRESENTLY AT SANDWICH ST. 24
LONDON
GREAT BRITAIN

Sophie can hardly believe it: a real letter from her Felix! Her heart leaps, and she clutches the letter tightly. Then she hugs Mom, takes a deep breath, and shouts:

"Lena, Nicolas, Julius, come look!"
When Dad comes home from work, he gets to read the letter too. "Hmm, hmm, hmm," he says, sounding surprised, "so the traveler has landed in London! That's the capital of England."
"How many people live in a capital?" Sophie asks. She wants to know all about where Felix is now.

With Dad she looks in the encyclopedia under *London*. It says there: "Capital of Great Britain and Northern Ireland, lying on both sides of the Thames River, population almost seven million, residence of the royal family. Contains about 1,600 churches and chapels, as well as fortresses including the Tower of London and the Houses of Parliament. One of the largest cities of Europe."

Dad points to a picture and says that the English queen lives there in the palace. Later in bed Sophie wonders whether Felix has seen the queen in the palace. Does she take her crown off at suppertime? Thinking it over, Sophie falls happily asleep.

Buckingham Palace

Palace guard

Tower Bridge

Tower of London

TO: SOPHIE
33 ELM ROAD
MANSFIELD, OHIO
U.S.A.

A few days later a letter arrives from Paris. Sophie sticks the envelope in her pants pocket, climbs up the old apple tree in the garden, and begins to read.

A LETTER FROM PARIS
FROM
FELIX

"Hmm," Sophie wonders, "how can everything be so different in Paris?" Then she remembers that Grandma is coming to visit this afternoon. She will know all about it for sure, since she has been to France many times.

"*Ooh là là*, the rabbit is in Paris," Grandma exclaims. Then she tells Sophie about the game Felix has described. It is called *boule* and is very popular in France. Sophie is interested to hear that Paris has a wonderful cathedral, wide shopping streets, beautiful gardens, and some very old churches. Then Grandma fishes out a travel guide. Sophie flips through it, and Grandma dreamily exclaims, "Oh, they have simply the most *delicious* food there."

As proof she serves a baguette, which is the bread Felix saw, cheese, and French salad. And it tastes almost like a trip to France.

Eiffel Tower

Sacré-Coeur

Champs-Elysées

Slowly it gets dark and it is time to go to bed. "*Bonne nuit,*" Grandma whispers in French when she comes to say goodnight to the children.

"Do you know how much longer Felix's trip will take?" Sophie asks.

"Now, that is hard to say," Grandma answers. And thoughtfully she adds, "Travelers always want to see just a little more."

Sophie thinks this over. "Does that mean that Felix will never come back?" Suddenly there is a big lump in her throat.

"Don't worry—Felix will be back home for Christmas. I am absolutely certain!" Grandma says quietly and gives Sophie a big good-night kiss. Instead of counting sheep tonight, Sophie counts the days until Christmas.

Just a few days later Sophie receives another envelope with Felix's squiggly writing.

MAIL FOR
SOPHIE
33 ELM ROAD
MANSFIELD, OHIO
U.S.A.

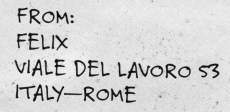

FROM:
FELIX
VIALE DEL LAVORO 53
ITALY—ROME

Spanish steps

Colosseum

Pantheon

Sophie can stop worrying now. Grandma really was right. Felix writes that he will be coming home. As long as she knows he's coming, it doesn't matter when! But what's this secret code? "Maybe Julius will know more about it," Sophie thinks.

She finds her big brother bent over a book, studying, and tells him about the letter from Rome.

"I know that secret code," Julius groans. "We had a vocabulary test on it this morning in school." He hands Sophie his Latin book. Most of the pages look very strange, but Sophie finds some pictures of the temples in Rome that she loves.

In the morning Sophie looks all the way up and down the street. But there is no sign of a little rabbit with a suitcase. "Come home, Felix," she whispers and hopes that her wish will come true soon.

Slowly the leaves on the trees turn color, and autumn comes. Sophie and her brothers and sister build four paper kites with Dad. On the weekend they fly them in a big field. Sophie waits every day for the mailman. She has already given up all hope of news from Felix, when the mailman finally hands her a colorful envelope. Immediately Sophie knows that it can only be from Felix.

CAIRO

5

NIL POST

19.10.

EGYPT

TO SOPHIE
33 ELM ROAD
MANSFIELD, OHIO
U.S.A.

MAIL FROM FELIX
PRESENTLY IN CAIRO
EGYPT

This letter Sophie reads twice. She just can't imagine the pyramids. How high are they really? While she is wondering, Mom comes into the children's room.

"Well, since our Felix is in Egypt now, I have a surprise for you," she says. Mom won't tell Sophie anything more, and it's still a secret when they get into the car and drive away. When Mom finds a parking place, Sophie sees a big sign. It says "EGYPT—an Ancient Kingdom."

Sphinx

In the Museum, Sophie is amazed. There are so many display cases, big pictures, and even an animated film. That afternoon she finds out how the pyramids and the sphinx were built.

When Mom and Sophie get home late that afternoon, Julius calls out, "Well, have you brought a mummy back with you?" Right away, Lena wants to know what a mummy is.

Nicolas wriggles his fingers and whispers darkly: "That is an old embalmed pharaoh that wants to come and get you!"

"Eeeee!" Lena squeals.

"What nonsense," Sophie says. "Don't believe a word he says. Pharaohs used to be kings in old Egypt."

"Exactly," says Julius. "They have been dead now for at least four thousand years!" That sounds better to Lena. Feeling better, she helps Sophie build the biggest pyramid made of blocks that has ever been in the living room.

KENYA
12.11.
MAIL

KENYA
AFRICA
8

MAIL FOR
SOPHIE
33 ELM ROAD
MANSFIELD, OHIO
U.S.A.

Sophie runs home fast one particularly rainy November day. When she gets in, she can't take her new rubber boots off fast enough— because there on the hallway table lies a crumpled envelope.

FROM FELIX
ON A SAFARI
KENYA
AFRICA

Sophie looks up from the letter. Fat raindrops splash against the window. Everything outside looks so gray. She can hardly believe that the sun could be shining anywhere in the world. The next morning it is still dark when Sophie takes a bus to the zoo with her whole class. Most of all she wants to see the elephants. Everything there is very quiet. Only an old zookeeper is there. He tells her that every year there are fewer and fewer elephants in Africa. "But why?" Sophie asks. "Isn't there enough room there?" "There's plenty of room," the zookeeper tells her sadly, "but unfortunately there are also too many people who ignore the hunting restrictions, and only think about getting the valuable elephant tusks!" Sophie is outraged and decides, "When I am grown up, I am going to protect the elephants in Africa!" That is her secret plan. She will tell it only to Felix when he is back home.

In the evening the wind howls around the house. Sophie snuggles up with Dad on the sofa. "Where can Felix be now?" she wonders. "I hope he doesn't catch cold."

While she is thinking, Dad suddenly asks, "What would you all say to baked apples? Who will help?" Sophie stirs the vanilla sauce. Nicolas fills the hollowed apples with almonds. Lena nibbles here and there—sampling, she calls it! As the apples sizzle in the oven, Mom asks mysteriously, "Can you guess who is coming to visit for Christmas?"

"Tell us who!" the children chorus.

Mom stretches out the mystery, staring at them slyly, and at last tells them, "Aunt Edda is coming!" Sophie and her brothers and sister are thrilled. Aunt Edda has been traveling all over the world. She tells exciting stories and is always full of new ideas.

Suddenly they smell something burning. "Uh-oh, save the baked apples!" Dad yells. But they get there too late.

"Don't be sad, Dad," Lena says. "We still love you anyway."

The day that Sophie and Mom bring the box of Christmas decorations out of the basement, a colorful airmail letter arrives for Sophie.

Sophie's heart leaps with joy: Felix must be already on his way home! Then she rubs her forehead, thinking hard. She has heard of skyscrapers before. But was Felix exaggerating about the big lady in the harbor? It doesn't matter—when her dear cuddly rabbit comes back home, her room will look really great. Filled with excitement, Sophie cleans up and sticks the Christmas star decorations on the window.

Empire State Building

Statue of Liberty

Then she hears Mom calling, "Children, come look!" Whenever Mom says that, something special is happening! Sophie runs out to the hall—and there stands Aunt Edda with her arms open wide. They hug and hug and hug—until at last Sophie lets Aunt Edda talk.

On her trip, Aunt Edda had seen lots of things; she had even been to New York! "What do you know!" Sophie thinks, and she asks her aunt about the big lady in New York.

"Oh, yes," says Aunt Edda. "She has a real name. She is called the Statue of Liberty." Then things get really exciting, because Aunt Edda opens her suitcase. She has brought little presents for everybody from her trip. Sophie actually receives a miniature Statue of Liberty. It is so small that Sophie can easily hide it in her fist.

That night Sophie and her brothers and sister are allowed to stay up later than usual. Together they look at Aunt Edda's photographs. Then Aunt Edda sleeps in their room.

When everybody wakes up the next morning, it has snowed a little. At last it is time to start baking Christmas cookies. It is dark outside by the time the five big cookie tins are filled to the rim, and the whole house smells like cookies.

Sophie knows Christmas is not far away now. Tonight she can hardly fall asleep for excitement. But day after day passes without hearing or seeing anything of Felix.

By Christmas Eve Sophie is doubtful. Maybe Felix was kidnapped or has gotten sick along the way? Wherever can he be?

Suddenly there is a knock on the front door. "Santa is coming," Lena whispers. "Sophie, go look!" Sophie's not afraid of Santa, who always looks an awful lot like Dad. She opens the door . . .

but there is no red hat to be seen. Sophie looks to the left and the right, and then at the doormat. She can't believe her eyes, because there—yes, truly—there stands Felix, with a small suitcase. "Felix, oh, Felix!" she shouts again and again. Sophie hugs her cuddly rabbit, looks at him, and hugs him again. Then she picks up his suitcase and sees it is covered with colorful travel stickers. Sophie shuts the door and whispers in his ear so that no one else can hear: "So, Felix the globe-trotter, now you must tell me exactly how you managed to travel around the world!"

His answer remains Sophie and Felix's secret. But if you want to know what Felix brought back from his world tour, just take a look in his suitcase!

家書 (P.37)